Plastic Back

Plastic Back

Anna Rakes

iUniverse, Inc.
New York Lincoln Shanghai

Plastic Back

iUniverse books may be ordered through booksellers or by contacting:

iUniverse
2021 Pine Lake Road, Suite 100
Lincoln, NE 68512
www.iuniverse.com
1-800-Authors (1-800-288-4677)

ISBN-13: 978-0-595-38543-0 (pbk)
ISBN-13: 978-0-595-82923-1 (ebk)
ISBN-10: 0-595-38543-5 (pbk)
ISBN-10: 0-595-82923-6 (ebk)

Printed in the United States of America

To Mom:
for helping me live this.

Contents

Not a Hunchback

For the seventh graders, like myself, at Benson Intermediate School (commonly called B.I.), it was scoliosis screening day. Woohoo. Just another reason to get out of class and hang out in the library until it was our turn to go into the back room with the parent volunteers. I thought this was such a waste of time, but I wasn't complaining. After all, it gave Kristin and me a chance to recap our Saturday night fun, which had involved talking to Ben, my crush, on the phone for hours about who was the cutest in the class. Throughout the conversation, my absolute best friend and I had written notes back and forth to each other about Ben, unbeknownst to the adored boy. We had masked our laughter the entire time. He'd had no clue we were drawing hearts around his name and writing our first names with his last name on the old notebook. And now another homeroom was ahead of us, so we had plenty of time to chat and glance back at Ben and giggle. I'm sure my face was red by the time they started screening my class.

Everyone knew the drill of the scoliosis check. Mrs. Sanders, my teacher, had briefly told us that parent volunteers were going to make us take our shirts off and bend over so they could take a quick look at our backs to check that we weren't all crooked. Of course we knew we were all fine—no hunchbacks in this group. Only freaks had twisted spines. The speedy exam didn't bother me at all; I knew the moms doing the screenings. Actually, I was more concerned about not being able to reach all the way down to my toes without bending my knees than I was about the back check.

Last week in gym, I'd once again failed to meet the standards of the President's Physical Fitness Test for the v-sit reach. Honestly, what did v-sit even mean? And it was such a dumb test: to have to put your feet against a box and stretch your arms as far as you could past your toes. I could play sports and pass all the other tests, but apparently, I was cursed with tight hamstrings. Oh well, I hoped I could carry on a conversation long enough that the mom examining my back wouldn't notice my bent knees.

"Next," I heard the mother say. I proceeded into the room and closed the door behind me. I quickly slipped off my T-shirt. The mom softly said, "Go ahead and bend down, honey." I followed her instruction while discussing how my father had back problems and my brother Cole had experienced some trouble with his as well. The woman quickly ran her finger along my spine, and then she laid both hands across my upper back, one on each side. Her examination didn't bother me; I was too busy concentrating on keeping my balance and enduring my throbbing hamstrings that kept me from quite touching my toes. All the while, I tried to continue the conversation as a diversion.

"Yeah, they say sometimes this stuff runs in the family. But you know, I mean, I'm straight as an arrow for sure…I bet you're tired of doing all these checkups today when, clearly, none of us have problems…"

"All done," she interrupted.

When she informed me the exam was over, I stood up and grabbed for my shirt, ready to race back out to gossip more with my best friend.

"Not so fast, Anna Beth. Actually, I'm going to recommend that you have a checkup with your pediatrician. It appears you have a rib hump on one side of your upper back. Just get it checked out. I'm sure it's fine. See you soon. Have a good day!"

Was she for real? What on earth? What did she mean, "rib hump"? I wasn't a hunchback! Geez, lady. Oh well, I'd tell Mom, a *real* nurse, and she'd take a look at it. This woman wasn't even a nurse. She was just some stupid parent volunteer with nothing better to do than check kids' backs for some freak curve they might have. Not to mention, she had looked at my back for what—all of three seconds? Yeah, like you could tell a person had scoliosis from *that*. Well, she'd made a mistake with me—I knew it.

After I told Mom about the screening at school, she looked at my back and agreed I should have it checked, just to be sure. She didn't see anything major except a slight rib hump across my upper back. She told me it was just a weird thing that had been on my back for quite some time and that no one had said anything about it before.

I went the next week to see Dr. Kane, my pediatrician. I knew he would give me good news. He'd tell me how dumb the parent was and how they needed to get real nurses in there checking people's backs. I didn't really care about this visit either—it was just another reason to skip school. And since my school was a good hour from the hospital, I missed most of the day. Nah, I wasn't nervous, but I was seeking revenge. I had this burning urge to prove that the mother had misdiagnosed me. Anna Beth was *not* deformed.

Dr. Kane did the same drill: he made me bend over and then ran his finger along my spine. His checkup proved a bit more involved, however, as he made me walk across the exam room. Standing straight and completely naked was, by far, the worst part. I felt like a weirdo walking stark-naked across a room as my doctor and Mom just watched from behind. How embarrassing for a twelve-year-old girl to have two adults eyeing your potentially curved back and your naked butt as you tried to walk as straight as possible. Now I understood how babies would feel, if they could think like that, when they're first born and lying naked while everyone stares at them through the glass window of a hospital nursery.

I did this naked walking drill several times, and by the third or fourth trip across the frigid floor, my toes were curling up, making it increasingly harder to walk straight. My toes squeezed together and I shifted my weight to the outer sides of my feet to ease the freeze of the unfriendly tile floor. After the embarrassment that happened next, though, I would have preferred the cold tiles. Dr. Kane decided he needed one more look at my spine while bending over. He instructed me to touch my toes. "Hah," I uttered under my breath. If only he knew I was as inflexible as a telephone pole. When I attempted to touch my toes, Dr. Kane noted my lack of flexibility.

"Are you stretching, Anna Beth?"

"Oh yeah, of course I do—especially before basketball. Yeah, I stretch before basketball all the time. And, um, speaking of basketball, did Mom tell you about how I am *so* good at point guard? I get, like, six steals a game. And, and I'm one of the captains, and, and if we win our next two games, we get to play in the county play-offs! You should hear my friends. They're, like, so pumped for me—it's really like the biggest thing they're talking about."

Basketball was my escape and he bought it. Dr. Kane sensed my embarrassment and quickly accepted my proud, rambling answer. I knew he was a basketball expert. For years he'd talked about his three children, all over six feet tall, who were excellent basketball players. After what seemed to be a ridiculously long checkup, Dr. Kane said I could get dressed. I quickly threw on my shirt, as fast as I had done in the back room of the library, trying to escape unwanted news of any possible problems. Once again, I was stopped before darting out of the exam room.

"All right, Anna Beth, it looks like, if you've got any curve at all, it's probably only about three degrees or so. You know, a lot of people have three-degree curves and have no idea they even have them. I think you're going to be just fine, but sometimes these things are tricky to see with the eye. I'm going to have you go upstairs and get an X-ray, just to be sure. We'll be able to see from the X-ray whether your spine is curved—and if we'll have to do anything about it, OK?"

"What do you mean, 'do something about it'? What would you have to do?" I impatiently questioned.

"Well, if it turns out that your spine is curved more than a few degrees, we might have to get you into a back brace to help you grow straight. But you'd go to a special doctor for that. And that could be a long way off, so there's no need in worrying about that now. Let's just see what the ol' X-ray has to say before we get anxious."

This was a shocker. I had no idea he'd say anything was wrong with me. For a second I felt a little guilty for writing off the parent volunteer's exam, but not for long. I was perfectly normal, and even if I did have a slight curve, it wasn't a big deal. I'd still be a regular girl. After all, he said a lot of people have small curves. I was tired of this back business. So for the sake of ending the entire saga, and because an actual authority said to do so, I left the exam room and headed up to the third floor to have my X-ray. At least I would have a cool story about getting an X-ray of my back, which few kids my age do. And more importantly, I couldn't wait to get to my game that night. We were going to kill those whiny girls from Jackson.

Hot Lava

During the excitement of the days following the X-ray, I completely forgot about the embarrassment I'd experienced earlier in the week. We killed the team from Jackson. And yours truly had at least three steals, but knowing me, it was probably more like eight. Like I said, I was good. Two nights later we beat Green Ridge in overtime to go on to the championship game. I'd told Dr. Kane we were awesome, and we were. With four seconds remaining and the game tied, I quickly dribbled up court and hit Becca, our top scorer, down low. She sunk a basket and we led by two. The last second clicked off the clock as Mary Ann, our tallest player, knocked away a Green Ridge player's inbounds pass. And that was it. I made the assist of the year! Of course

Becca scored, which was awesome. But more importantly, I once again proved my amazing assist skills and we were headed to the tournament final. For the third year in a row, we would face Glenville, our biggest rivals. And it was all because of my stellar ball handling and court vision. So what if I couldn't do the v-sit.

Aside from the game, there was so much going on at B.I. that week. Coming up in three weeks was our first dance of the year, the Fall Ball. I could not have been more pumped. The only other dance I had been to was the sixth grade graduation dance. Now, let's be honest. That was far from cool compared to what this one would be like! Everyone was constantly talking about what they were going to wear and who they wanted to dance with. And, of course, I couldn't wait for a chance to slow dance with Ben (whom I had been in love with since kindergarten). Sigh. That would be too perfect: a championship game and a slow dance with the cutest guy at school.

Mom picked me up from school. And on the three-minute drive from B.I. to Cole's school, Kennedy Elementary, I babbled all about the game and the dance and how I wondered what song my boy and I would get to dance to.

When we pulled into the parking lot, I realized we were five minutes early. Excellent! Plenty of time to finish unloading all of the most important details of my current junior high life on Mom, who looked a little spaced-out. Somewhere in between talking about slow dancing to "Wonderful Tonight" and my perfect assist, I noted how glad I was that I was *finally* out of that baby elementary school.

"That school was so lame," I claimed, rolling my eyes and dragging the word "lame" out as long as I possibly could. "People in junior high are *so* much cooler than those stupid kids at Kennedy. Man, am I glad I'm done with that place." Quickly I jumped back to potential first kisses and the new outfit I had to have for the dance, but Mom seemed far from excited. She kind of stared off in space and just slowly nodded at my thrilling recap. It was somewhat disappointing; I had waited all day to recount my cool life to her and she looked as if she was off in a world far from inside our white Ford Taurus.

Finally, I guess when she'd had too much of seventh grade talk, she interrupted, her voice struggling to be calm.

"Anna Beth, I got the report from your X-ray today. They measured your back and you have not one, but two curves." She paused. "And they aren't three degrees. They're twenty degrees each."

I was as stunned as I would've been had Ben actually asked me to dance. My God, what had happened? I was supposed to be laughing when Mom told the moron mother that she had been wrong about my back—not hearing that I had two twenty-degree curves. What did that mean?

"Do I have to get a brace?"

I gulped so loudly that it sounded like I tried to do it on purpose, but I didn't. She said she didn't know and that we were going to have to go to an orthopedic specialist to find out what the next step was. Excuse me—an *orthopedic* doctor? I thought about how I couldn't even spell that word (even though I had been the school spelling bee runner-up two years ago). And though I kind of knew what it meant, because Cole had been to one of these special doctors two years ago, I was still confused.

For the first time in the seven-and-a-half minutes we had been in the car, I sat still and quiet. Thoughts of Ben's arms resting on my hips and of me making the most beautiful pass for the winning bucket fled my mind. My thoughts were filled with hatred for that dumb mother and her letter home saying I needed a checkup. Having to walk across the freezing floor naked while people stared at my behind disgusted me. I was sickened by that stupid X-ray—that one picture of my bones that would forever change my life. I mostly hated this nasty news that interrupted my mile-a-minute narrative of junior high life. Bottomless hatred gushed through my veins like hot lava; It was so fierce that I didn't even hear Mom's attempt to soothe me. I could kind of see her mouth forming the words "It'll be OK, baby. Don't worry," but it was as if I never even heard them. Only when Cole opened the door and gave his usual goofy "hey guys" greeting did I return to the present, hearing world. But I was still.

The Tightrope

I was thankful for the arrival of my brother, for his slamming of the car door, and for the silliness in his voice. For a second I felt a pang of envy for my brother's innocence. Even if he was still at a school with five-year-olds, at least he wasn't old enough to endure the scoliosis screening and all that it had entailed. His intuitive mind and the uncertainty he saw in the faces of two people whose facial expressions he knew quite well clued Cole in to the presence of something beyond the three people in the car. Mom told him in as few words as she could about the recent news. He nodded awkwardly and patted my shoulder from the backseat.

What an awesome brother. In that minute, I hated that it was me who was going to endure whatever was to come, but I appreciated his undeserved kindness. I constantly downed him and his experiences, reveling in how much older I was than he. It was funny how, in that moment, our fourteen-month age difference seemed much less than I usually tried to make it. The rest of the drive home was fairly quiet, and so was the remainder of the night. I felt so angry. "Why the hell did I deserve this?" I uttered after my prayers as I fell asleep that night.

The next morning, I felt somewhat better than I had the day before and busied myself with packing for school, brushing my teeth, and eating a sandwich. I hated breakfast foods. I despised runny eggs and sticky syrup-covered waffles. Chicken salad on regular white Merita bread was my morning choice, and I stuck with tradition. On the way to school, I contemplated whether I would tell my friends about the trip I would take to the orthopedic doctor's office in two days. I decided to hold off simply because I wanted to seem as normal as possible—certainly not like some hunchback freak. I agreed with myself to stick to talking about Ben and the upcoming dance.

The first day after I had gotten the news passed quickly. I stayed committed to my contract with myself and didn't mention the twenty-degree curves, the orthopedic doctor, or the possibility of a brace. At lunch, Kristin and I sat together. Only once did she ask me if everything was OK. Other than that, it appeared that nothing seemed abnormal to her. I whispered about how cute Ben looked in his hat and how I wished that, when he walked up to the jukebox to play a song, it was already the dance and he was playing a song for us to dance to. (The lunchroom jukebox was one of the best parts of B.I.). He played "My Maria" by Brooks and Dunn, one of my favorite groups. Actually, their concert was my first. I was in fourth grade at the time. I even shook Ronnie Dunn's hand. Maybe it was fate that we both liked Brooks and Dunn. Unfortunately, Ben sat back down with a beautiful girl named Maria, and that was that. It wasn't fate today.

Just as the disappointment sat in, Kristin saw her crush dump his tray. She rambled on and on about Andrew, a guy the whole school wanted to date—even the eighth graders. She blabbered on about how tall and athletic he was and how cool he dressed. Everyone wanted to go out with him. Kristin wasn't the only one spending her lunchtime sighing over him.

Aside from lunch, we didn't have many breaks to just sit and talk during the day, so I was safe from spilling my news. The five minutes in between classes was barely enough time to get your locker open, switch books, and walk to another class. It certainly wasn't enough time to unload potentially life-changing news on one of your best buds. Before I knew it, I was home and back in the comfort of people who knew my secret. Thank goodness. Kids with something wrong with them didn't usually fare well at school, especially in junior high. Although there was the rare exception, like when someone got colored bands for their braces.

Rather than being made fun of for it, a lot of kids with color-coordinated braces, at least those who were popular to start with, received attention because of their new accessory. But at other times, a physical change spelled doom at junior high. All it took to determine one's fate was the willingness of only a few people to think the new thing cool. There was this weird fine line that required a flawless balancing act between being a freak and someone who was unique and cool. For junior high, the ultimate goal was to be different enough to be considered distinctive and popular, to just stand out above everyone else, but to not be so dissimilar that you lost the unique title and were referred to as weird or freakish.

Two days later, on the morning of my orthopedic appointment, there was quite a buzz at school. As soon as I got off the bus, my friend Jessica ran up to me and asked if I had seen Lindsey's glasses.

"Anna Beth, you *have* to see them. They have a cool, hippie-like pattern on them and they make Linds look *so* much older!"

Andrea quickly jumped in and shouted, "A.B., I can't wait for you to see them! Her glasses will be *perfect* for the dance to go with Lindsey's new outfit. Ahh, this is so exciting!"

Of course Jessica and Andrea thought the glasses were cool—they had the worst fashion sense ever. I constantly tried to give them outfit advice; but they always seemed to end up wearing the same old stuff. Andrea even had this rotation of shirts she went through every week: blue, white, green, stripes, and plaid. Every single week Andrea wore those shirts in that order. It didn't surprise me at all that they were so ridiculous over Lindsey's glasses, but I figured they were overreacting as usual. Poor

Linds; glasses were so annoying. At least two people thought they were cool though.

Right then Linds strutted around the corner with her new glasses that everyone was *ooh*ing over. I was shocked to see four of our other friends literally hanging on Lindsey as they all walked down the hall together. It was just like a typical scene of the most popular girls in every teeny-bopper movie ever made. I complimented Linds on her glasses but wasn't nearly as excited as everyone else. Our friends thought she was even cooler with the glasses than before. Never had our crew hung all over Linds. Usually they were hanging on me. I expected Jess and Andrea to act this way, but certainly not the rest of my girls. I guess they thought the new facial accessory was unique and not "loserish." Even though I was somewhat jealous, I had to give Lindsey props. At that moment, I was witnessing a successful acrobat, walking ever so gracefully across her tightrope.

My appointment was scheduled for one thirty that afternoon, which meant I got to leave school and all the ridiculous hoopla over Lindsey's glasses just after lunch. When the bell for second lunch rang, I felt my stomach groan even though I wasn't particularly hungry. I knew what lunch would bring—Kristin, Jessica, and the other girls all *ooh*ing over Lindsey's glasses. Lucky for her they liked them. Lindsey could've just as easily fallen off the social ladder that day, but instead, she climbed several rungs. Whatever. I had more important issues to worry about. My stomach twisted and growled at my secret fear—that I'd have to wear a brace, and that it wouldn't be as well received as the glasses. After all, there didn't seem to be anything hip about a brace—at least nothing as cool as flowers on funky glasses.

Over the past several days, I'd researched online what these braces looked like. Needless to say, they were anything but comfortable looking. The images that came up when I searched the Internet for "scoliosis braces" were of huge, bulky plastic contraptions with thick metal bars that went up around your neck like a stiff dog collar. The body part of the braces was made of thick plastic and looked like a full cast that stretched from your neck down to your thighs. I squirmed in my chair when I thought about trying to wear baby doll T-shirts with one of those things. Impossible. These braces looked worse than the horrid corsets women used to wear years ago. When we learned about them in social studies, I wondered how on earth women tolerated wearing those things. And now, I might have to wear something even worse!

I thought that the talk of Lindsey's glasses would last for the first couple minutes of lunch and then move on to the dance or our upcoming game. Nope. It went on well beyond a few minutes. Even after devouring my disgusting, rectangular cheese pizza and the poor lettuce and tomato salad, my stomach was still not satisfied. I was sick of hearing about Lindsey's dumb glasses. I had far more significant things on my mind—like the appointment that afternoon and, more importantly, the prospect of having to wear a brace for the rest of junior high and high school. I couldn't imagine parading down the hall wearing that huge apparatus. My neck would be stretched out like a hideous ostrich, and I'd be doomed to wearing sweatshirts for the rest of my adolescent years. Certainly, no one would be hanging off my brace or drooling over it like they did Lindsey's glasses. Didn't they know how silly they looked doing that?

But I knew why it seemed so dumb to me. Of course I wanted to be Linds. Who wouldn't have wanted a bunch of popular girls announcing the extreme coolness factor of your new specs? The girls made the glasses out to be the best new accessory we'd seen in weeks—at least since Sarah's Sharpie marker key chain, which had created a stir for at least four class periods. I was jealous of their appreciation for Lindsey's glasses and secretly thought about the brace that I might have to wear. I was sure that if I had to have it, I'd long for them to find my less attractive brace equally as compelling. And they wouldn't. They would probably talk about it a lot, but mostly behind my back, making fun of me. Whatever. Maybe the brace wouldn't turn out to be so bad. I mean, what if they thought it was semi-cool, like Lindsey's glasses? I know at first she wasn't thrilled about having to get them. She whined about it for over an hour the night before she picked out the frames.

Linds worried that she wouldn't be able to hold her social balance and would fall out of the popular group, thanks to her bad eyes. I understood her fear because it was the same dread I had that day during lunch. But, oddly enough, they liked her glasses. And maybe if I had to wear a brace, it'd turn out like Lindsey's glasses, and I'd end up getting more attention than I did before. What if Ben actually started hanging out with me because he thought it was cool that I put up with that brace and that I was different? It worked for Lindsey; why not me? All of a sudden, my stomach muscles loosened at the prospect of an even higher social standing.

And in that moment I did it—I was sick of hearing about those dumb glasses and needed everyone to understand that I had a much more pressing issue—I blurted it out.

"Yeah, well, guess what. I might have to get a back brace for scoliosis." I couldn't believe it. I'd said it. Everyone stopped and turned to face me, their mouths dropping open. And Kristin cautiously asked,

"What? Anna Beth, what did you just say? OK, OK...go slow and tell us what's going on."

They seemed concerned. Not thrilled or excited or even like they'd like me more. No, they were weird—really quiet and worried. Not the response I wanted. They didn't squeal or link their arms with mine and giggle. They didn't say, "Ooh, Ben will think you're super strong for that." They didn't ask me what it would look like or even why I might need the brace. No, they didn't repeat the news by shouting across the lunchroom. Rather, their mouths slowly dropped open and they stared. Their silence was worse than words.

But I was in too deep. I had to keep talking. Their serious eyes were all fixed on me. I fell deeper and deeper into my story, wishing I had never started it. "Turns out my spine is really curved and I, I actually have two curves, so my spine is in the shape of an S." Kristin slowly nodded, Sarah's head tilted slightly as her lips tightened, Jessica remained motionless, and Andrea covered her mouth with the classic "oh no" face.

I nervously continued, "Yeah, so, this afternoon I have to go to this really special, like important, doctor, who only deals with critical patients, and he has to figure out what's going to happen and, um, what they're going to do about it. But it looks like I might be wearing a brace for it, which would be really serious and such a big deal, but I know I could deal with it. You guys know me—I'm so strong and, like, I can so deal with whatever. No biggie."

Sigh. There it was. I had said it all. And they just looked so stunned. My best friends hadn't bought my story or my false excitement about the condition. And rather than *ooh*ing, they *ohhhh*ed. Kristin, sitting right beside me, threw her arms around me and buried her face in my shoulder.

Jessica solemnly said, "A.B., this really stinks. I'm so sorry!" And I wondered what had happened. This wasn't a funeral, and I surely wasn't dying. I didn't want sympathy, at least not this kind of sad, moping pity. I wanted someone to say that it might be cool to have a brace like that. Or that it would be awesome, like the corset in the social studies book. Or that now someone could punch me and it wouldn't hurt me, like a bulletproof vest. I yearned for laughter, not stares. And mostly I longed to shove my secret back in my mouth. I prayed Ben would get up to play a song, even if it was for Maria, so we could all drool over him like normal. The motionless, glazed eyes staring at me made me want to shout about how cool Lindsey's glasses were and how perfect they'd be with her new skirt for the dance. But I didn't. Instead, the bell rang. Lunch was over.

A Perfect S

The hour-long drive to the doctor's office seemed like a blur. By the time we turned onto Post Drive and saw the big building on my right, I had forgotten even driving over. The sign read "Valley Orthopaedic Center." I finally saw how you spelled the horribly long word. I now know, of course, that the word can be spelled two ways, but then, the *a* just confused me and looked very misplaced—as misplaced as I felt pulling into the parking lot.

The waiting room was filled with broken legs and crutches. There were people everywhere with visible problems—people who looked like they needed to be at an orthopedic, excuse me, *orthopaedic* center such as this. Not me. They had no idea what was wrong with me.

One girl my age stared at me the entire time I waited. A cast covered her broken arm from wrist to elbow. I almost wished I had some visual justification like that to represent my presence there. But I didn't. I figured she was sitting there wondering why a perfectly normal and healthy preteen like me would be here in this rather depressing place.

It seemed like it took forever before they called my name. I watched some boring video about eating healthful foods and taking daily calcium supplements that played on a small TV in the waiting room. When the film started repeating itself, I switched from that to guessing people's injuries. Finally, I just thought about the championship game that was two weeks away. If I did end up with a brace, how would I ever have any more amazing assists? Who would get Becca the ball? And how would the team win without their captain?

"Deanna, you can come on back."

The words halted my thoughts of the game and directed my attention to a slim woman in a white nursing dress and rather old-timey hat. She didn't even know my name. I was Anna Beth, not Deanna, my given name. I had never gone by Deanna except once in fifth grade when I wanted to be cool and more grown-up and decided to change my name. The name change had never actually stuck. I had been in the same school since kindergarten, and my friends just didn't know me as a single-name kind of girl. The nurse's failure to address me properly soured me even more on the whole experience. I followed the woman anyway as she led me back to a room. I mostly rolled my eyes at her stupid hat as I walked behind her. Mom was a nurse and she certainly did not look as dorky as this woman, who looked like she'd stepped right out of a *Dick and Jane* book. Mom wore funky-colored scrubs and wouldn't have been caught dead in a hat like that. She would've complained about the pins hurting her head and probably would've never accepted a job that required her to wear such a foolish accessory. Mom was cool.

The room we entered was extremely tiny. It had one stool on wheels, a cot-like bed, and one chair. I sat on the edge of the vinyl bed and Mom sat in the chair by the door. The nurse with the useless hat instructed me to undress and put on the gown that she pulled out of a tiny cabinet, the only other piece of furniture in the room. Fantastic, I thought, more nakedness. I prayed this visit wouldn't include a naked strut across the room while my mom and the new doctor just stared. I felt like the room was too tiny for that. There was barely enough room to take a couple of steps in there, so I decided the possibility of the naked catwalk routine was slim to none.

The nurse left, and Mom helped me tie the back of the gown. The gown swallowed me and, even when tied, the gaping holes in the back offered glimpses of my butt. The nurse knocked and told me to come with her to be x-rayed. I wadded up the excess fabric of the gown and held it in my left hand as I walked so no one behind me could see through the holes. We paused at a scale and the picture-book nurse told me to hop on up so she could get my height and weight.

"Eighty pounds exactly, and, let's see, you're fifty-four inches tall; that's four feet six inches," the nurse informed me as she recorded the data on her clipboard.

Now I know that doesn't sound like much for a stellar basketball player, but remember: I was the point guard, and I excelled at ball handling and defense. Actually, it was my small stature that allowed me to steal the ball so much. I was too quick for any of those bigger girls, and I would sneak up on them and take the ball before they knew it. I wished I could prove my skills right then, but instead, I followed the nurse into the X-ray room.

"Tina will take it from here. She'll do the X-ray. When she's done, head on back to your room. Dr. Miller will look at the X-rays and then come talk to you."

Thank goodness. At least I was done with the overly smiley nurse. The X-ray involved Tina, the technician, putting a heavy shield around my neck. It draped over my shoulders and would "cover my breasts." Hah! I wondered what breasts she was talking about. I supposed I would be a late bloomer like my mom, and that was OK to me, but there was no need to talk about something that wasn't there.

Unfortunately, the breast comment wasn't the most surprising remark Tina made. Next, she asked me if there was any chance I was pregnant. Yeah, right. "No, Tina," I said. "I haven't even started my period yet." Though Tina didn't have an annoying hat, she apparently had the task of directly calling attention to my underdevelopment. Thanks a lot, Tina. As if I didn't feel self-conscious enough at school in the locker room when we changed into our gym suits. All of the other girls had something to fill their bras. I, however, wore a tiny sports bra—not because I needed extra support during physical activity, but because it didn't have actual cups—perfect for someone who needed to cover a flat surface. I longed to tell Tina about how I led my team to the championship game and how it was my assist and great point guard play that guided us to wins in all but one of our games.

But when I looked around, Tina was out of the room, staring at me from behind a window. As I opened my mouth to describe my amazing skills on the court, Tina's voice came through a speaker. "Breathe in and hold it," she said. I followed her instruction. After a groan from the machine in front of me, followed by a buzzing sound, Tina reappeared from behind the window and removed the shield.

"Go on back to your room, Deanna, and have a great day!"

I clutched the gown and walked back to tiny room number sixteen, annoyed again by the incorrect name. When I opened the door, Mom jumped up and started in with countless questions: "How was it? How much did you weigh? Did she measure your height? Do you think the

X-ray tech did your X-ray right? How did she have you stand? Did they shield your chest? Did you hold your breath so the picture wouldn't come out fuzzy?"

"Geez, Mom, calm down."

"I can't, Anna Beth, I'm so antsy. I've already peed twice since I've been waiting here for you to come back."

"Good grief, maybe we should be getting your bladder checked instead of my spine," I replied sarcastically. That was the most annoying part of Mom being a nurse: she knew too much. She questioned and overanalyzed everything anyone said about my condition.

After Mom's initial questioning came the most boring part of the whole experience. I swear we sat in that room over an hour before the doctor ever showed up. I practiced my stretching for a while, placing my legs up on the exam table and loosening my hamstrings, all in the hope that I could make it through the exam with no comments about my inflexibility. I felt like I did that day in line at the library—worrying that I wouldn't be able to touch my toes. I remembered the v-sit and the stain it had put on my record for the Presidential Physical Fitness Award. I hated that stupid test, but I was grateful for these thoughts. They replaced my fear of what the doctor would say.

Later, I spun around on the stool with wheels, sliding back and forth across the tiny room. Mom mostly gnawed on her fingernails and said stuff like "You better get off that. He'll be here in a minute, I bet." And of course, she was right. My new doctor walked in as I was taking one final glide across the room. Assuming my riding device was his seat, I hopped up quickly and returned to the exam table.

Dr. Miller looked like a walrus. He had a full and somewhat puffy mustache that covered all the space between his nose and mouth. It kind of curled over his top lip, and I thought about how I bet it bugged him when he ate. He could've used a trim. From then on, I could think of him as nothing but a human likeness of the large marine animal. For the most part, with the exception of the standard old-man hair on the sides of his head, Miller was bald. His head was shiny all the way down the center. I was glad he didn't have a comb over. That would've been as hideous as the nurse hat. The new doctor laughed a lot and was quite friendly, introducing himself the second he came in. Miller called me "Anna Beth," which I appreciated more than ever. Overall, he was an upbeat guy and I was glad. Usually when people had bad news, they didn't sound so happy. I assumed, because of his tone, that I was in the clear as far as the brace went.

After an introduction and a few minutes of get-to-know-you talk, Miller slapped his hands against his knees and cheerfully said, "Well, let's take a look at your back here. Why don't you bend over and touch your toes for me." The doctor untied the gown and ran his finger along my back, just as every previous examiner had done.

"Can you bend any further? A girl your age ought to easily be able to touch her toes."

I started to blurt some impressive basketball stats to once again hide my tight hamstrings, but instead I strained with every ounce of grit I had and, finally, my middle finger brushed my big toe.

"There ya go. OK, now come on back up and have a seat."

The new doctor patted my back as he wheeled around to the X-ray viewbox on the wall. At this point Dr. Miller described how we were going to look at my film and see what we had on our hands.

And there it was. It looked like the letter S. In fact, it was the most perfect S ever. My spine bore the exact shape that Mrs. James, my first grade teacher, used to write on the board for us to emulate. Each curve was equal and they balanced each other out—like two crescents, sitting one on top of the other. The walrus explained how the equality of these curves, twenty degrees each, caused me to look straight to the eye. Fully dressed, and even naked, no one could tell I had a textbook S spine.

I was worried. There was no time anymore for jokes, and Miller didn't care about my stupid basketball skills. For the first time ever, I didn't want to tell anyone about them either. I wasn't thinking about the dance, or Ben, or writing notes during our phone conversations. Now my head was filled with what-ifs: What if I never got to play basketball again? What if I even had to have surgery? What if I had to wear a brace and it looked like the pictures from the Internet? For once, I simply sat and listened.

"The best thing for you, Anna Beth, is going to be a back brace. The brace will help you grow straight while you go through big growth spurts during puberty. Likely, you'll wear the brace for about four years. It'll be extremely important that you wear the brace as much as I tell you to, or your curves will get worse. And then you might have to have surgery."

Like a frying pan to my face, his words banged against me. I was motionless. I doubt my eyes even blinked. The worst had come true. I continued to listen.

"Now, the great thing is, they've improved so much over the past twenty years or so, and really the braces aren't that bulky. They're a really light plastic. You can't even see them under clothes really, and especially since big T-shirts are so in style these days, you should have no problem hiding the brace under your regular clothes."

I thought there was nothing "great" about this at all and resented him for saying that. It was easy for him to sit there and tell me that it wouldn't be so bad because the braces weren't that bulky; he didn't have to wear it. Even if they were a little lighter and didn't show through as much under clothes, we were talking four years here—that was all of junior high and half of high school. And who was he trying to convince that big T-shirts were in style? Maybe for guys they were; but clearly the ol' walrus had no idea what was cool for a seventh-grade girl to wear. Oversized T-shirts were definitely *not* what I had in my closet—so much for baby doll T-shirts and miniskirts.

I still sat motionless. I looked up at the X-ray again. My brow furrowed and I slowly shook my head in disbelief at the ugly S I saw shining through the lighted box on the wall. This wasn't happening. It couldn't. I buried my head. I thought about how I'd have the brace for the rest of the time at B.I. and how I'd still be wearing it on my first day of high school. I'd even have the brace when I learned to drive! Driving a car seemed like such a long time away; I couldn't imagine having to deal with the brace until then.

I felt Mom place her hand on my crooked back. I sort of zoned back in to what she and Miller were saying. Mom rubbed my back and stroked my hair. According to Miller, I could still do regular activities even with my brace on. And if I went swimming, I didn't have to wear it at all. Mom told him about how I played basketball. She said it, not me. I'd still be able to play, but it would be harder, he said. At least I still had basketball. I had to get a grip on myself. I told myself that I was so strong and could deal with anything. And just as I started feeling like I might be able to tackle this plastic beast, the worst news came. My new doctor also said I'd have to wear the brace twenty-three-and-a-half hours a day. That meant all the time—to school, to sleep, to games, and to dances. I could only leave my brace off while I took showers. Four years was bad enough, but all day and all night for four years was nearly unbearable.

I left the doctor's office feeling completely stunned. I didn't have tons of stories to tell about the constant goings-on of junior high and, instead, remained quiet on the way home. Once or twice I think I muttered that I was sure wearing the brace wouldn't be that bad. I just kind of sat there, not knowing what to think. As we turned onto the interstate, Mom told me I could go without wearing my brace until after my final game. I guess maybe she didn't want me to be hindered in any way at one of the things I did best. Maybe she just felt sorry for me. Or perhaps she thought an hour or two wouldn't really make that much of a difference. My body felt numb. I wasn't that scared, nor was I crying over this terrible card I had been dealt. A brick could've fallen on me and I wouldn't have flinched. I just sat.

The next day at school, I didn't care what everyone had to say. I felt like their hugs and "Oh, I'm so sorry, Anna Beth, this is really awful" comments were empty and fake. What did these people know? They had no idea what sitting in a tiny room staring at a picture of your perfect S felt like. My friends were clueless about the embarrassment of not touching my toes and the internal agony of thinking about how uncomfortable that brace would be. They were ignorant of everything I had endured during the past day or two. I went through the daily motions of school, but no jukebox songs made me emotional. And I didn't engage in talk about the dance at lunch. I never once even bragged about the upcoming game.

While making it through that school day was terrible, things at home weren't so bad. Thankfully, Mom and Dad didn't say much about the brace that afternoon. And Dad, my coach, got me back in the playing mood. We shot around on our home court. And during dinner, when everyone was at the table, he talked over and over about how great my season had been and how, without me, we wouldn't have been in the championship game. I appreciated his effort. And it did sort of make me feel better, but I didn't brag about how fabulous I was or shove it in my brother's face or in anyone else's. The truth was that I wasn't that great. Heroines didn't have plastic backs.

Cole just made me laugh with his stupid jokes. Thank God for him. I could tell Mom and Dad just tried to cover up the pink elephant in our house, but Cole was genuine. He wasn't trying to make things seem all right. I think deep down he knew I'd be fine. In fact, he just might've had more confidence in me than I ever had in myself. Instead of buttering me up, all night he asked me stupid questions that previously had only annoyed me.

"Hey, Anna Beth," he'd say in his goofy voices. "Which would you rather do—drink the juice from the bottom of a garbage can or lick the floor of the school bus?"

These repulsive inquiries were my saving grace. They made me laugh and grit my teeth, all at the same time. Mostly, they kept my mind focused on serious decisions—like choosing between trash juice and bus crud—and not on my twisted back.

The Shell

The plastic curse was tight. It was a hard shell with an opening in the front. I was instructed to slide into the brace, breathe deep, and then tighten it. I followed directions: sliding in, breathing deep, and tightening the three Velcro straps across the front. I couldn't get a good breath in though. And it was so snug against my ribs that they were sore after a couple of minutes from being jammed against the hard plastic brace. My shell came up over my chest. Yep, all the way up over my nonexistent chest. Even though I didn't have a chest to speak of yet, I feared this plastic shield would stunt any future development. But it didn't just come up over my chest; it also pushed up under my arms. The brace dug into my armpits and shoved my shoulders up, making me look like I had sewn the shoulder pads of the 1980s in all of my shirts. When I looked in the mirror the first time I wore the brace, I looked beefed up, as if I had put on weight to play football or something. I didn't even try on my baby doll T-shirts—big shirts it was. So much for style.

After I successfully got the brace on, I bent over to grab my purse and the Velcro pulled, making a crackling sound from under my shirt. Fantastic. I couldn't wait to be crackling all day long. I mean, there's nothing like the sound of rubbing Velcro. As I stood up, I looked in the mirror to see the lower butt portion of the brace poking out from under my pants. See, the brace hit my butt mid-cheek and created a ripple in my butt when I stood up straight. And when I bent over, the edge of the brace stuck out. Sigh. It was exactly what I wanted in junior high—a rippled butt and linebacker shoulders.

When I sat down in the car to drive home with my new accessory, it dug into my thighs. I had never been so uncomfortable. Every time I turned even the slightest bit, the brace dug into my skin and restricted my movements. After being in the car for about five seconds, I was roasting.

"Mom, seriously, please turn the AC up! I'm burning up in this thing."

"Anna Beth, it's already freezing in here. What's wrong?"

"What's wrong? Are you kidding me? I'm strapped into a plastic corset over here. I can feel the sweat pouring out of my body into this stupid tube sock I've got on under here. I think it's already soaked! I need *air*!"

I immediately learned that the worst part of the brace was how hot it was. For the rest of the car ride home, even though Mom had the AC blasting, I sat roasting in my shell. When we got home, I found no reprieve. Even though we kept our house thermostat on about 68 degrees, I was sweltering. Mom's advice was to sit on the couch and relax, which I tried but couldn't do because I was in too much discomfort with the plastic monster cutting into my legs. Finally, at bedtime, I found my only source of comfort. Even though I wasn't used to sleeping on my back, in bed I was lying flat where no part of the brace could dig into me. The brace was miserable.

I fidgeted on the entire ride to school the next day. I was nervous about my first day back. What would they think of the brace? Would it be like Lindsey's glasses? I doubted it. But would anyone even notice the brace? I had no idea how they'd react.

At first, no one said anything about it. Then, in the locker room during gym class, the girls all crowded around me. It wasn't a crowding around and shouting out about how cool my brace was, like they had done with Lindsey's glasses. This was an "Oh, A.B., I'm so sorry" and "That thing looks awful" and "Does it hurt?" moment. The girls felt sorry for me, and I could tell their concern was genuine, but the brace still didn't make me cool. They didn't think I was awesome for going through such a hard thing— I certainly wasn't a heroine. They just felt bad for me—kind of like how they felt sorry for the kids in Special Ed. It was concern, but not envy, like they had for the glasses. Just as I had figured, I immediately lost my social balance.

Still, I didn't mind telling them all about my brace. In fact, talking about how huge of an undertaking it was made me feel like I was really dealing with something hard and important. But the more I said, the worse my friends felt. In gym, the v-sit was the least of my worries. I couldn't do any of the warm-up stretches, and I wondered how I'd ever loosen my tight hamstrings if the stupid brace kept me from even barely bending over. I sat out for the second v-sit reach test. And only in getting excused from the test did I feel even close to how Linds must've felt with her glasses.

When I got to record everyone's scores instead of actually doing the horrid v-sit, some of my friends talked about how lucky I was that I had a brace and didn't have to do the dumb test. Hah! As if having a brace were lucky. I did like it though when they acknowledged my uniqueness with the brace. I enjoyed some sick pleasure when marking failing scores on the record sheet for my classmates who couldn't reach far enough. But even though I didn't want a low score on the test, I was envious that I didn't even have a second chance to improve it. No matter how hard I tried to enjoy marking the scores, or how much I giggled inside when someone failed miserably, deep down I would've rather missed the mark at the v-sit than have to stand there and not be able to at least try it. Instead of letting anyone know about my conflicting feelings, though, I usually agreed with my friends and seconded how standing there with the clipboard and pencil was far better than ripping my hamstrings to reach across the ends of my toes.

On the fourth night of having my brace, we played in the championship game. I got to finish out the season brace free, but we lost for the third time in a row to our archnemesis in the final game. We were down by two points in double overtime with only seven seconds left on the clock. Becca was open for the perfect shot. Jess threw the ball inbounds to me, and I dribbled a few times before launching the ball down the court to Becca. She caught the pass and took a shot beyond the three-point line to win the game—we were sick of always tying, and none of us had the strength for a third overtime. The ball bounced off the rim and a Glenville girl rebounded right as the buzzer sounded. That was it. Maybe Becca should've taken a two-point lay-up. The lane was open, and she could've probably tied and sent us to triple OT, but I honestly just didn't care.

Before the brace I probably would've been furious. I'd have gone on and on to all my friends about how great my pass was and what a dumb move Becca made. But at the end of the game, in some way, I was glad the season was over. Maybe it was because I wouldn't have to weigh the options of whether or not to wear my brace for any more games, or perhaps I was just tired of keeping up my basketball-star image. After all, I was only a point guard. And I only played county-league ball. Losing a game wasn't awful; and Becca wasn't to blame. Tying was getting old. We were both tired.

Fake Legs

That Friday, Kristin came over after school and we picked out my outfit for the dance. Of all of my friends, Kris understood about my physical problems the most. Before last year, she was an awesome soccer player. She played on a boys and girls team, and even as an elementary kid, she had gotten the attention of the junior high coaches who had come out to watch her. Everyone knew Kris would start on the B.I. team as a seventh grader and would probably play for the high school as an eighth grader. She was that good. But at the end of her sixth grade season, Kris fell on the field and broke her leg. Ever since then she hadn't been able to play—the healing had been a really long process. The doctors told her it'd take a long time to build back up to where she was. So, even though her broken leg was a shorter-term problem, she kind of knew what I was going through. Her cast had been annoying the whole time she had worn it.

Kris helped me find an outfit that my plastic shell didn't show through, and we dressed for the dance. Kris had brought her outfit with her after school because Mom was taking us together. We didn't want to show up alone and have to walk around aimlessly looking for friends. We wanted to get there at the same time so we could giggle about our guys when we saw them. We literally shoved our spaghetti into our mouths and guzzled down some Diet Cokes before screaming at Mom that we were ready to go. After one last mirror check, I decided my green and purple plaid skirt and my purple top looked great. No brace showed through, and I still looked hip and cute. Kristin was a lifesaver. I knew we'd have the best time ever.

People were already jammed into the cafeteria when we arrived. The room was hot when we walked in, but it didn't really bother me because it was also dark. Dark was good. It was just how I had imagined it: a dark room with a few lights spinning, great music from the DJ's stand, and ahh, there he was—Ben. Yes, Ben had been a vital part of this dance daydream. There he stood with his nice khakis and blue button-up dress shirt. The sleeves were rolled up a little and the top buttons were undone so his white T-shirt showed through. He looked perfect. I stood there kind of stunned before Kristin grabbed my arm, linked it with hers, and started walking. Thank God she made me move or I would've continued standing there drooling over him.

We paraded through the crowd, stopping to talk to our best buds and compliment them on their outfits. I continuously looked over my shoulder to keep tabs on Ben. I didn't want the night to pass without dancing with him, and I especially didn't want him to get too much time with Maria.

After an hour or so of standing around talking and awkwardly dancing in a group of girls (and by dancing I mean uncomfortably swaying back and forth), my friends started to break up and go dance with boys. We squealed under our breaths every time a guy came over and asked one of our girls to dance. After Scott came and led Sarah onto the dance floor, I looked up from my giggling circle of friends and met eyes with Ben. Just then, we looked right into each other's eyes. He smiled that perfect smile of his where one side of his mouth started a sort of cocked, flirty smile that then moved across his lips into a full blown smile. I grinned back, walked out onto the floor, and met him. Neither of us said anything; we just started dancing. I put my arms around his neck and he placed his hands on my waist. He immediately said, "You're wearing that brace thing aren't you? I can feel it."

My face reddened and I stumbled through the words, "Yeah. I can only leave it off for thirty minutes a day, so I had to wear it."

"Oh, that's cool; I just felt it on your waist. So, this is *way* better than our sixth grade dance, huh?"

And just like that, he did it. He acknowledged my brace and avoided any awkward moments of each of us understanding how weird it was that I felt hard, like a turtle, under my clothes. But he also moved on from the topic and just smiled as we chatted about how far superior this dance was to our elementary school dance. It was fabulous and perfect, and even though the song wasn't "Wonderful Tonight," it was just as good. I was even glad it was a different song, because I was different now. And I was glad Ben was OK with that, even if we were just friends.

The dance with Ben ended all too quickly. He didn't know how much it meant to me. I didn't really even care whether he liked me anymore (of course it would have been *awesome* if he did, but his friendship was great too). In the moment of dancing with him, all of my frustrations, anger, and embarrassment over the brace had sort of lifted. All I could think about was how long I had dreamed of that dance and how kind my boy had been. After Ben, I danced with a few other friends who said nothing about my brace, but didn't make the moment awkward, either. So far, the dance was great! I looked around for Kristin. I didn't see her and figured she had left to dance with other people when I danced with Ben. I started surveying the room, looking for her.

All of a sudden, Jessica interrupted my search and said, "You're dancing with Andrew; come on."

I couldn't believe it and thought she was joking as she dragged me across the floor. Of course, my boy was Ben, but Andrew was simply unattainable. As I said, all the girls wanted him—especially Kristin. Andrew was dancing with

Molly, a girl in Special Ed. who always followed him around. She constantly professed her love for Andrew; and we all just kind of chuckled about it. Somehow, she tracked him down at the dance and made him slow dance with her. He was staring in my direction as we approached. He raised his eyebrows at me and motioned with his head for me to come over. Like an iron statue, I stood stiff and still until Jess dragged me over to him. Jess quickly pulled Molly away and informed her that her dance was over. At the same time, Andrew grabbed me and pulled me to another part of the dance floor.

I felt horrible for Molly. At the same time, I knew Andrew didn't really want to dance with her, so my sympathy for her quickly left. I was afraid Kris might be really mad if she saw me dancing with her boy. But it was Andrew! How could I pass up the opportunity? I couldn't. In a matter of seconds, he swept me to a corner of the room and started dancing with me. Our dance was short because it was mid-song when I intervened. Really, we only exchanged names and talked about what classes we had and who our friends were. He never mentioned my stiff waist, and since he wasn't a good friend of mine and didn't know I had a brace, I wondered what he thought of it. After the dance, we parted, and I didn't expect to talk to him again. After all, he was the most popular guy in school—and I was the back-brace girl.

"Are you upset? I'm so sorry, Kris. I, I don't know. It just all happened so fast, and the next thing I knew, we were dancing. But it was only for half a song; and I didn't start to like him or anything like that. And, and I thought about you and was worried the whole time you'd be mad at me," I rambled once we were back home.

"Nah, I'm not mad. I mean, sure, I wish I had danced with him, but I think my days of liking him are over. I danced seven times with Alex, and he is *way* more fun than Andrew. And I think he's really cute, too..."

I was glad Kristin didn't hate me over Andrew. It was just a silly dance anyway—the only reason he wanted to dance with me was because he was with someone worse. Later that night, during the post-dance gossip session, Jess called me. Kris and I were just sitting there, laughing hysterically about Andrea kissing Matt after the dance and cutting his lip with her braces. Hahaha. How embarrassing. I hoped Jess had even more hilarious stories that we'd missed.

"He said *what?*"

"He called me and asked if you had fake legs that were attached at your hips, because your waist was so hard," Jessica answered as she laughed.

"Why are you laughing? This is *so* not funny!"

"Oh, Anna Beth, lighten up. I thought it was pretty hilarious."

"OK. Well...I guess...anyway, I've gotta go. See you Monday. Bye."

I hung up. I was mortified. The hottest guy in school thought I had fake legs! He'd probably go and tell all of his popular friends that I was a freak. Kristin gave me a huge, silent hug. She knew she couldn't say anything to make me feel better, and I appreciated her for not trying. For the next few weeks at school, I tried to hide myself, keeping my head down in the hallways—like a turtle that had crawled back into her shell for a while.

On the Home Court

Despite my extreme embarrassment, I tried to forget Andrew and the whole "fake leg" syndrome. Luckily I didn't hear anyone at school mention it, and three weeks later, I was back to playing ball on my home court.

I called Kristin and told her she had to get over to my house as soon as possible—Travis was there! Kris and I both thought Cole's friend Travis was adorable. He had the shiniest, smoothest black hair. And though he was small in stature, his dark eyes and amazing basketball skills made him ever so appealing to us. We loved it when he came over! All we did was flirt with him when he visited.

Cole and Travis played on the same basketball team, and when Kristin's mom dropped her off at my house, they were outside shooting hoops. Kris ran up to my room and we devised a plan of how we'd go out there and start playing with them. Cole rolled his eyes when we walked outside and I held up my hands, motioning for him to pass to me. I knew what he was thinking, and he knew why we were out there. He shook his head and just kind of laughed to himself, letting me know it was OK even though he wasn't thrilled at our presence.

We just played pick-up ball, so it didn't matter if the brace kept me from running well—our court was barely the size of the key. Playing out there was fun—there was no pressure, nothing was at stake, and I didn't strive to be the heroine. We fouled each other unmercifully, and when we were tired of that, we decided to make up plays. We practiced our plays for hours on end, as if we were college or professional teams preparing for huge games. All four of us tried as hard as we could to do our part on these plays. And when we finally felt like we had them down, we made Mom come out and videotape us to memorialize our greatness. These plays consisted of a couple passes and a lay-up. But to us they were groundbreaking, and we had no problem spending all afternoon perfecting them.

I couldn't remember when I had laughed as hard as I did that afternoon. We had so much fun. Except for the moments when I got to guard Travis and brushed against him, I was completely relaxed. After the film session, we decided to do our usual dunk contest. Kristin and I brought out the small chalkboard I had used when playing school as a little girl, and we set it up as the scoreboard. Of course, we girls never participated in this; it was a contest just for the boys. We had far more fun scoring them and being in control of the board. Plus, I couldn't touch the rim, even with the goal at its lowest height. The contest required both of the guys to do three dunks, and we judged them on how good the dunk was overall and, also, in other categories, like "form." But the real reason for these contests was so Kristin and I could flirt with Travis. Cole was awesome, and we had been playing with him for years, but these contests gave us a chance to attach scores to the boys, and our sly way of flirting with Travis was to always give him the highest score.

Obviously, we did not want to appear biased, so we each came up with an individual score to give both guys. This way we could vary them some—but Travis always came out the winner. We gave Cole some lame award, like "best style" or something, just to make him feel better and to make it less obvious that we favored Travis. But the boys were smarter than we thought; Cole laughed every time the scores were revealed.

Kristin left after the dunk contest because it was time to pick up my new piano. Even though I was in seventh grade and most people started lessons when they were much younger, I decided to take piano lessons. Mom thought it would be a good idea since basketball was over. It was also something I could do inside in the air conditioning. I'd played trumpet in the band, but I hated it. I was good at the trumpet when I first started playing in sixth grade, but in the summer before B.I., I got braces on my teeth and it messed up my whole playing ability. I had to learn how to hold my mouth all over again. Plus, the metal mouthpiece and my braces smashed my lips. Practicing the trumpet actually hurt; I hoped the piano would be less painful.

And it was. I loved piano. I practiced constantly and enjoyed learning new pieces and playing for my teacher every week. Sure, I wasn't playing the most advanced stuff. I mean, I started out learning "Happy Birthday". But it was fun and I stayed cool. I could play piano even with a shortened running stride. And it didn't matter that I had shoulder-pad arms, because I practiced in my living room by myself.

The Wing

Physical fitness testing was over in gym and we had started football—perfect for the cool, early November weather. Kristin and I were pumped about football. We loved the sport and went to many of the high school games with our parents. It was always so much fun, except that, no matter which parents we went with, they all made us sit with them in the stands. A lot of our friends were allowed to walk around the track and stand together behind the bleachers, near the concession stands. This was where the most extreme gossip went on, and everyone wanted to be there. But we had to stay up in the stands unless we went to the concessions, then we had to come right back. Football was football though—gossip circles or not—and we loved it.

Football in gym class was way different than watching games on Friday nights at the high school. But it was still fun. In gym, we played flag football: each person had a belt with two colored flags, one on each side. "Tackling" someone meant ripping off one of their Velcro flags. One thing that was good about football in gym was that you didn't have to run too fast—people just kind of moved in a pack—so I was good with my short stride. Plus, there was no bending or stretching.

Mr. Dillard, my gym teacher, counted us off in teams. Kris and I smiled at each other when we saw the teams were coed and that we didn't have to play just with girls. Previously he made the girls play with the girls, and the guys with guys. This was no fun because most of the girls weren't any good. Kris and I were really athletic and competitive, and we wanted to actually play—not just stand around until Dillard came over to get everyone moving. On another day, we had fiercely grabbed a few flags off girls we didn't like much. Kris even tripped one of them. It wasn't so bad. But today's coed teams meant we could get out there and rough up some of the other girls and strut our stuff in front of the boys, too. Plus, the guys loved it when a girl caught one of their passes or scored a touchdown. Guys always circled around girls who actually did something worthwhile in the game, and Kris and I were determined to have that be us today.

No one except the center and quarterback really had positions. Everyone else kind of lined up and ran toward the end zone in the hope that someone would be open for a wobbly pass. Our team received the ball. Scott, one of the fastest kids in our class, caught the ball and took off running. He was unbelievably quick and we all just jogged behind him, watching him fly ahead with the ball. A kid pulled Scott's flag when he was only fifteen yards or so from the end zone. We had almost scored on the return! This was so awesome. We were going to kill the other team.

Josh, our QB, threw the next ball to Sarah, but she didn't run quite fast enough and the ball went over her head. I felt sort of bad for Sarah because she wasn't a fast runner, and I knew what that was like with my brace over my thighs. But we still had three tries to score. We huddled up and Josh revealed our plan, "OK, let's try to actually make a play here. Anna Beth, you go wide on the right side here, and everyone else, run left. I'll toss the ball to her and she can run it in."

"All right," we said, agreeing as we tried to catch our breath.

"You got it?" Josh asked, looking at me.

"Yep. I got it."

"Break!" he shouted as he clapped his hands together and broke up the huddle.

I couldn't believe it! Why had he picked me? I bet he thought no one would expect me to get the ball, but the reason didn't matter. I was pumped and so ready to make our first TD. When Cory snapped the ball, I followed my instructions. I ran to the far right side of the field and up just a little before turning around to look at Josh. He threw the ball and I lunged for it with my arms out, in hopes of scooping it up. The ball fell right into my hands. I turned and ran as fast as I could toward the end zone. Even though the brace was pressing against my thighs, I ran with as big of a stride as I could, pressing toward the goal. From the corner of my left eye, I could see Jessica coming at me from the side. She grabbed my flag just before I scored. I slid on the grass a little before regaining my balance. I dropped the ball, but it wasn't a fumble because she had already snagged the flag. I didn't make the TD, but I'd brought us much closer, and I was thrilled.

"Good job, A.B.!" Kristin shouted.

"All right, all right. Nice, Anna Beth!" yelled Josh, "Now throw the ball back over here."

My smile was huge. I was thrilled at the encouragement, especially from Josh, a guy I barely knew. But as I bent down to grab the ball and head back over to my team, I heard it. Just like the ripping sound of the Velcro flags from the belts, the straps on my brace crunched and rubbed. The Velcro crackled as I bent over, and I feared the straps would rip apart. But the Velcro held the front of the brace closed.

As I reached for the ball, though, the back of my brace split. The tough plastic ripped apart. There was no loud crackling sound like the Velcro straps. Rather, the tear was nearly silent. I could feel the top of the brace loosening its grip on my chest; the further I bent over, the deeper the tear traveled. I couldn't believe what was happening. Because there was no sound to the cracking brace, I really didn't even know if it was actually happening at first. But when the plastic armor was no longer pressing against my ribs, I knew I wasn't just imagining things. The tear went only halfway down the back of the brace, so it didn't completely fall apart. But when I stood up, the ripped plastic jutted out from under my shirt, as if I were growing a wing. I wished I had grown wings so I could've flown far away from the football field and from all of my friends staring at me. I couldn't move though. I just stood still.

I saw Josh chuckle to himself, covering his mouth with his fist. Jess laughed the same laugh I had heard the night she called with the comments from Andrew. Other people just stared at me. Kristin was the only one who moved. She ran over and put her arm around me. Kris grabbed the football from my hands and hurled it back over to Josh, and then she escorted me to the locker room. I waited until I passed everyone on the field before I released the tears. My face flooded with streams of embarrassment and humiliation. I could feel the broken brace flapping against my shirt the entire time we walked. I could only imagine what everyone on the field was saying. Kris and I remained silent until we got inside.

I had caught the pass and my friends cheered me on. They'd welcomed my success and were excited. I was happy, too. But that stupid brace had to ruin everything. It spoiled basketball and made me a slow runner. It caused me to sweat and to have damp skin all the time. It created the ripple in my butt and embarrassed me at dances. Because of it, some people thought I had fake legs. It shoved itself into my armpits and made me look like I wore football pads under everything. And now, it took away my success in football and embarrassed me in front of all my friends.

Kristin comforted me, "Anna Beth, I know you're really upset. But everything *will* be OK. I'm sure that's the last thing you want to hear right now; but you will be all right. I know you, and you are strong. And we will get through this."

And she was right. That was the last thing I wanted to hear. But coming from Kristin, it was OK. I knew she was sincere and would stick by me no matter how many times the brace humiliated me.

"Let me help you take the brace off, at least for now. Do you want to call your mom?"

"Yeah," I whispered

"OK, let's take off the brace and go to the office to call her."

Kristin was an amazing friend—the only one who would walk over to me on the field. I recognized her strength and was grateful for her.

I ripped the Velcro straps apart and slid out of my brace, dumping it on the locker room bench. I stared at it with disgust. The rip started at the armpit and traveled diagonally through the upper back portion, stopping in the middle of the brace. I wanted to grab it, split it apart, and finish the tear. I gritted my teeth as I thought about finishing the job. I dumped my backpack and stuffed the brace in there. Kris zipped my bag while I put my gym shirt back on. My face was red and splotchy all over. That always happened when I cried. I even got splotches on my forehead.

We walked to the office. Kristin kept her arm around my shoulder as we moved through the halls. A couple times, I looked up at her when we passed other people. She glared at them for looking at my splotchy face.

Mom said I could keep the brace in my locker and not wear it for the rest of the day. Honestly, I didn't really care what she said. I wasn't going to wear the broken shield anymore that day. What good would it have done anyway, flapping under my shirt? It certainly wasn't holding me straight and tall. I tried to dry my eyes before getting ready for my next class, but the more I thought about my stupid brace, the more the tears flowed. I hated that brace. I hated every-thing about it—especially its wing.

The Girl with the Plastic Back

After school on the day of cracking my shell in PE, Mom took me to a brace repairman. He fixed my brace by adding plastic and making it thicker—not exactly what I'd hoped for. Extra plastic made me worry that the brace would be even more visible under my oversized clothes. I dreaded more than ever going to school the next day. Mostly, I feared PE and the football game I knew I'd have to play. How could I ever face my friends and especially my enemies on that field after cracking in front of them the day before? At least Kristin would be there.

Despite my worry about PE, I couldn't lose too much sleep over it. My mind was on other things. Not only would the next day bring my return to the football field, but, more importantly, my piano lesson. And I still had a lot of practicing to do.

Unlike my friends' piano teachers, Mrs. King was especially strict. She taught piano full time and had twenty-some students of all ages. She was tough on everyone. Our teacher didn't just give us a talking-to when it was obvious that we'd failed to practice—Mrs. King gave out stickers for how well lessons were played. Now, these weren't smiley faces or apple stickers like our teachers at school give out. These said "Excellent," "Very Good," "Good," and "OK." It was clear to all the students that these words correlated with school letter grades: an Excellent sticker was equivalent to an A+, and an OK was a C at best. Not only were individual pieces graded, but she also evaluated our overall preparation and performance for each lesson. It was intense, like having another class after you got home from B.I.

And to make it even more like regular school, Mrs. King had an honor roll that she announced every two months. She'd described her honor roll system to me at my first lesson, when she'd taken a photograph of me sitting at the piano bench. "Now, Anna Beth, if you make honor roll, which means you've prepared and played well at each lesson, this photograph will be placed with the other honor roll students' pictures on the corkboard. And when we have our final concert in the spring, trophies will be awarded to the top piano student and to the student who is the runner-up."

Though the honor roll sounded intimidating, and I was only a beginner, I became determined to have my picture make the corkboard. Mom and Dad never had to tell me to practice. I practically lived in the formal living room, where our piano was. I played my required pieces over and over, and I constantly tried to find harder things to play on my own. The honor roll would be mine.

My current urgency to practice, though, was because the first honor roll of the year was to be announced the next day, and I was dying to see if my picture was on the board. Even though the honor roll had already been determined, I wanted to look especially prepared and on top of my piano game for honor roll announcement day. On the way home from the brace repairman's shop, I blabbered on and on to Mom about how nervous and excited I was over the next day's lesson.

As soon as we arrived back at home, I went straight to the piano and opened my assignment book. I practiced all of my pieces over and over and over. It didn't matter that they were simple or that they almost never required both hands to play at the same time. I worked at this music like I'd be playing it for an audience of thousands. These assignments might as well have been Chopin or Bach.

Midway through my practice session, Mom came into the living room and curled up on our oversized love seat, which sat across from the piano. Since I began taking lessons, this had become one of her new favorite spots. I didn't really know whether she just felt bad for me about the brace and having to switch from sports to music, or if she actually enjoyed listening to me stumble through the beginner music. Regardless of her reason, she was there.

"Oh, Anna Beth, that sounded wonderful," she praised when I finished playing the first piece with no mistakes. "You know, Anna Beth, I think it's so amazing that you just started taking lessons and you're already this good. I'm just so impressed. And the stuff you're playing isn't easy."

I appreciated her continuous praise, but her ear was untrained. After playing through my second assigned piece, she said the same thing.

"Wow, that was great! You are so good, Anna Beth."

Of course, I'd screwed up the timing on the eighth notes throughout the whole thing, but she had no idea. I always slowed down when I got to those. I started out fast and then couldn't keep the time when I got to the quick notes.

"I keep messing up the timing, though," I sighed as I set up my metronome to help me keep time. I hated using the beeping device to keep me on beat. When I used it, I knew I wasn't getting it right. And the sound of it detracted from the sound of my playing.

"Well, I couldn't even tell it, Anna Beth," Mom answered, trying to give me a boost. "I really didn't notice it. It sounded good to me."

As I sat the ticking metronome on the piano next to my sheet music, I looked out the window. There Cole and Travis were, making up basketball plays. They were running around our court, laughing and sweating. I looked back at my music and continued to play.

Mom stayed until dinnertime and listened to the rest of my practice. And even though the next day was the honor roll day, I didn't practice any more that night. After all, three hours was a lot.

At school the next day, I was all aflutter about my piano lesson. I just had to get through the day, and then I'd head straight to the lesson. My piano bag in my locker was a reminder of the big afternoon ahead of me every time I changed books. At lunch I chatted on and on to Kristin about piano and how much I loved it and about the honor roll. I'm sure she got sick of hearing it. But she listened and was genuinely excited for me.

"Anna Beth, that's awesome! You are *so* going to have your picture on that board. I mean, come on, you've been in piano for barely any time at all, and you're already playing good stuff. You practice, like, all the time. Every time I call your house, that's what you're doing. You never even answer the phone anymore because you're, like, *always* practicing." Kristin's reassurance calmed my anxiety,

"I know, I know. I'm just so excited!" I answered. "Enough of me. What's up with you these days?"

"Well, I couldn't wait to tell you! Get this, A.B., Alex asked me if I would go with him to the high school basketball game this weekend...His older brother is playing in it, and Alex wants me to go! Can you believe it?"

"Ahh! Kris, I am *so* pumped for you. That's awesome. You guys are going to have so much fun! It's, like, your first date. Oh my gosh! What are you going to wear? We have to plan what you're going to wear and say. This is so exciting!"

"I know, I know. I can't wait. But it's not a date. I'm sure we'll have to sit with his parents. And he didn't even call it a date...Oh, whatever, who am I kidding? It is my first date! Do you think he'll try to hold my hand? What if I talk too much and he thinks I'm annoying? What if his parents don't like me? What if..."

The bell interrupted Kristin's freak out about her date with Alex. We grabbed our backpacks, dumped our lunch trays, and headed into the hall for the rest of the afternoon. I was really excited for Kristin. She liked Alex a lot. I knew she'd have so much fun. I was glad something so cool was happening to her. We continued chatting about it all the way to our lockers.

Our lockers were far apart, so Kris and I parted ways long enough to exchange our books. I jiggled my lock and it finally opened. As I bent over to open my backpack and take out my books, I heard laughing behind me. "Yeah, that's her," I heard a boy say. The voice was familiar, but I knew it wasn't coming from a close friend. I stood up and turned around. It was Andrew.

"Excuse me?" I said.

"Oh, nothing," Andrew answered. "Just telling Matt here that you're the girl with the fake legs."

Where was Kristin? My heart pounded. Crap, she was still at her locker. I panicked inside. What do I do? And then I looked at Andrew and remembered the Special Ed. girl he wouldn't dance with and why he'd danced with me in the first place. I thought about how he'd called Jess to ask her if I had fake legs and how she'd called me to share his hurtful words.

"You know, Andrew," I said in almost a whisper, "for your information, it's a back brace." My voice grew stronger. "I have scoliosis. Do you know what that means? Probably not. It means my spine is curved twice, in the shape of an S. So if you're going to make fun of me, refer to me as the 'girl with the plastic back'—not the one with fake legs. At least get it right."

Andrew just stared at me and said nothing. He looked at Matt, and they looked at the small crowd that had gathered around. He barely nodded his head, pressed his lips together, and walked up the hall.

I finished exchanging my books. As I closed my locker, I turned and saw Kristin standing beside me. She smiled and put her arm around my shoulder. I smiled back.

Together, we walked up the hall to our next class.

The rest of the day flew by. Before I knew it, I was getting in Mom's Taurus and heading to my piano lesson. On the way there I told her all about Kristin's date with Alex. The piano studio wasn't far from the school and we arrived in minutes. "Come on back," I heard Mrs. King say as I shut the door behind me. I walked in and glanced up at the corkboard. There I was—a straight and tall Anna Beth, sitting at the piano.

A Different Road

The Thanksgiving piano recital was my first, and I was incredibly nervous. Mrs. King held our concerts in a big auditorium at a local college. I'd practiced on the piano there two days before, but I was still anxious. The piano was a grand piano that sat up on a huge wooden stage. Rows of seats faced the lone piano at which I would sit, in front of tons of people, to play my first piece for a crowd. It would be nothing like playing in front of Mom in our living room.

Mrs. King required us girls to wear long dresses so we would look professional on stage. She didn't want any short skirts riding up anyone's legs during the show. After all, we were playing classical music for the most part, and this was a big deal—we were playing at a university! I put on my long white dress. It came down to the middle of my shins and had maroon and dark green flowers all over it. Dark green was my favorite color. Mom had even bought me a dark green piano bench cover. My favorite part of the dress, though, was the material that came up around my neck, like a choker. I thought it was the coolest thing—a built in accessory. I felt so professional in my dress. I slid my shoes on, pulled my hair back in a ponytail, and went downstairs to practice one last time.

My piece was short, but it had to be memorized for the concert. I played it once with the book, just for a refresher, and then once through without. I hit all the notes but one, and my timing seemed pretty on target.

When we arrived at the concert hall, the other students were all seated along the first two rows of seats. Mrs. King's students were of all ages. I fell somewhere in the middle. There were some really little kids that looked like they were preschoolers and a couple of adults. Mostly, everyone was a little bit younger than me. I found my place and reviewed the program. I was going seventh. This was good because it gave me a little time to relax and read through my music one last time (I brought my book with me), but not too much time to sit there growing anxious. I opened my book and laid it on my lap. I positioned my fingers on my book as if it were the keys and played through the piece on the book, checking for any mistakes. Time passed quickly, and before I knew it, the first four performers had completed their pieces.

The next two students were boys a couple of years younger than I. Both boys played their pieces perfectly. They performed complex classical music and, as they rocked back and forth while playing, resembled professional pianists—the kind I'd seen on TV. These guys moved their fingers so fast and played so many keys at once. I didn't know how they moved up and down the keyboard so fast. I had played for a couple of months now and almost never played four keys at once. They were incredible. I clapped loudly for each of them. After they both finished, it was my turn.

"Next we have Anna Beth," announced my teacher.

I was so grateful to hear my name the way it was supposed to be said. I smiled, placed my book in my chair, and walked up the rickety steps to the top of the stage. I sat down at the piano and took a long breath. My teacher had advised us to take a breath before we began. I was a little bit afraid that my Velcro would crunch when I did so, but it didn't. Thank goodness, my brace held tight.

As my teacher announced my beginner piece, I looked out into the crowd. The stage lights were bright, so it was hard to see; but despite the glare, I could make out Mom, Dad, Cole, and Kristin. They were clapping just a little louder than everyone else. I grinned. I didn't care if the crowd could see my brace poking out as I situated myself on the bench. I even took an extra breath before beginning without thinking about a possible crunch. Then, I placed my fingers on the starting keys. I had shifted paths and was beginning a journey down a different road. But I had some very special people walking with me.

Author's Note

As a twelve-year-old girl wearing a back brace for scoliosis, I never thought I would write a book about my experiences. In fact, I never even wanted to remember the horror of the plastic nightmare. But now, ten years later, I understand the lifelong implications of an uncomfortable brace that developed my character and taught me the value of loving, supportive people. To be sure, it was embarrassing, restricting, and hurtful in so many ways, but the experience of growing up with scoliosis is a story that I want to share so that you, too, might realize the worth of loving friends and family and the growth that comes with any hardship.

I urge you to support and encourage your family, friends, and those who you barely know. Stand up for people you care about when they need you, and be strong when they cannot. Your love, friendship, kind acts, and acknowledgements mean more than you will ever know. Laugh with each other, especially when you face struggles. I suggest this to you only because, without this kind of support from my family and friends, traveling this road would have been much more difficult.

To Mom: your support and love, along with your loyalty to stay by my side, helped me through this trial and so many others. To Dad, Cole, and Kristie: your strength, jokes, support, love, and presence eased the frustrations of these tough times. In your own ways, you each helped me survive. I love all of you more than you'll ever know. To Bart: though you were not in my life when I lived this, I am eternally grateful for your encouragement and belief in my ability to tell the story. Thank you, and I love you. To my huge family and all of my friends who have been a part of my experience, to all of those who shaped the characters included in this book, and to those who I've met along the way, I thank you as well. I would not be able to tell the story without you.

One final note: While this book is based on my personal experiences, and though many of the events described here actually happened to me, the book does contain some fictional characters and events. Therefore, it is simply a work of fiction, based on my past.

978-0-595-38543-0
0-595-38543-5

9 780595 385430